KWAKU ANANSE THE ANTICHRIST- A BIOGRAPHY OF THE NEW AGE KING

Richard Kofi Armah

Published by Richard Kofi Armah, 2024.

KWAKU ANANSE THE ANTICHRIST- A BIOGRAPHY OF THE NEW AGE KING

First edition. February 6, 2024.

Copyright © 2024 Richard Kofi Armah.

ISBN: 978-1738305148

Written by Richard Kofi Armah.

Table of Contents

This Book is Dedicated to Mother Earth.

Chapter One
Introduction

THE HIGH COUNCIL OF Avalon has received a report from the New Race Commission on Planet Asase, indicating that the newly created race of human beings, known as the Greyman Being, is now sufficiently numerous. The time has come for Asase to enter its era of light, with these beings, formed from the genetic materials of both Greys and Asase's humans, serving as the biological uplifters.

FOR MILLENNIA, THE Race Commission has diligently worked on the creation of the Greyman Being. Contributors among human beings, who provided their genetic material, reported being abducted by the Race Commission from Avalon.

THE GREYMAN BEING AWAITS in anticipation within their garden, poised for the day when they will coexist with both Greys and Humans. The angels celebrated this news with joy, having long expressed concerns to the Universe Authorities about the lack of spiritual progress among Asase's human beings, who have tended to focus on weaponry, dominance, and internal conflicts.

NOW THAT THE NEW RACE is formed, attention shifts to the chosen leader tasked with guiding Asase into the new Age. This leader is anticipated to be the long-awaited Messiah, known as Kwaku Ananse. While some may see him as a savior, others may perceive him as the Antichrist. A high Avonal son, well-versed in such matters, was selected for this crucial role. The arrival of Kwaku Ananse, born on Asase and carrying the soul of the Avonal as his higher self, marks the beginning of a transformative journey for the planet

Chapter Two

The Evil Forest

K waku Ananse returned from the farm to meet his tribesmen, who were gathered at the chief's palace. A misfortune had befallen the Osono clan of Asase: a strange sickness had sent five people of the clan to their graves within hours of their having fallen ill.

ONE OF THE VICTIMS was Kwaku Ananse's one and only son, Ntikuma. Kwaku Ananse broke down in tears when he heard the shocking news of his son's death. He had never before wept so deeply. The clan members all gathered around Ananse to console him, but no one was able to stop the tears from flowing from his eyes, which kept up for hours. Ntikuma was the only nuclear family member that Ananse had in Asase, so the boy's death was a very big blow to the father.

THE ENTIRE CLAN WAS living in fear of this strange phenomenon. They didn't know who was going to be the next victim. Just a month ago, the entire township had suffered from crop failure when locusts descended from nowhere, invading their farms and destroying the entire maize farm belonging to the Osono clan.

THE CHIEF OF THE OSONO clan in the land of Asase addressed his people and assured them that their god would intervene in a timely manner to arrest the situation.

KWAKU ANANSE, WHO HAD joined the gathering during the chief's address, left the meeting grounds and headed to the oracle of the god of the Osono clan to determine the specific cause of the menace that was bringing this series of misfortunes to his people. At the oracle, the god, through his priest, informed Kwaku Ananse that the origin of the disaster was the evil forest in the land of Asase.

KWAKU ANANSE WAS FAMED as a great farmer and hunter. He had two pets that had been with him since his descent on the land of Asase as a newborn child. He went nowhere without these two pets, Mens Mentis and Emovere.

KWAKU ANANSE MADE A decision only after consulting with Mens Mentis, and he acted only when Emovere propelled his body to do so. Mens Mentis and Emovere had become like animal-gods to Kwaku Ananse. Mens Mentis analyzed an issue presented to him through Kwaku Ananse's senses, and then later presented his analysis to Kwaku Ananse so the latter could take a decision. When Kwaku Ananse expressed his will in the form of a command, Emovere picked up the command and thence commanded Kwaku Ananse's body into action.

KWAKU ANANSE THEN SAID in his heart, I shall meet the Devil face-to-face and we shall see which one of us perishes.

EMOVERE THEN SPOKE: 'Feel how passionate you are for the welfare of your people? Feel how angry you have become? Go and defeat the Devil.'

KWAKU ANANSE THEN SAID to the priest of the god of the Osono clan, 'I will enter the evil forest and destroy the Devil, and I shall replace the sorrow in our land with joy.'

THE PRIEST OF THE ORACLE said, 'We have lost enough souls in this evil forest, and we are loath to sacrifice any more. Think deeply about the decision you will take, for no one has ever entered the evil forest and returned alive. The day that you take the first step into the evil forest shall become your last. I speak not for myself, as I am just a vessel.'

KWAKU ANANSE CONSIDERED the warning of the priest, yet Emovere said, 'Let's proceed to the evil forest.' Kwaku Ananse then left the shrine and headed to the chief's palace, where the chief and the people had gathered in mourning for those lost. He bowed before his chief and announced his decision to embark on his fateful journey. The chief and the elders of the town became very troubled of heart when they heard his words.

THE CHIEF ROSE FROM his seat and headed to his room, saddened by the fate that he thought awaited Kwaku Ananse in the evil forest. The people became confused and distressed when their chief left their midst without explanation. Kwaku Ananse then addressed the people, saying, 'My people of Asase, I have decided to pursue the Evil One in the forest. I shall return with his head in my hand. And that shall symbolize the end of our suffering.'

THE CROWD'S DISMAY was apparent. One among them spoke for them all, saying, 'Do not leave us and perish in that forest, which takes so many of the brave and the wise among our people. Please stay with us, for we do not desire even one more of our kind to perish. We beg you to stay, brave son of Asase.'

After conversing with Mens Mentis, Kwaku Ananse spoke to the crowd. 'My decision I have already taken, and I am not looking back. All I need from you now is your prayers. I am no longer counted among the living; my name is already recorded in the book of the dead.'

HAVING SPOKEN, HE BEGAN to move in the direction of the evil forest, when the chief of his clan emerged from his room and spoke. 'Brave young seeker of the unknown, you cannot face the Devil without these,' he said, handing him a bow and a full quiver. 'You shall need them when you come face-to-face with evil.'

KWAKU ANANSE ACCEPTED the bow and quiver, and thanked the chief. Then, the chief's mother, matriarch of the Osono clan, spoke. 'Brave son of our land, without strength you cannot use the bow and arrow should you come face-to-face with evil. Take with you this food and water, for you shall need them before your journey's end.'

AFTER THANKING THE queen, he accepted the gift of mangoes, bananas, pineapples, and oranges, and a gourd containing water. He wrapped them all in a cloth and tied it to one end of a long stick. Then he hung the bow on his shoulder and tied the quiver to his waist. The blacksmith gave him a freshly sharpened sword.

KWAKU ANANSE CARRIED the food and water tied to one end of the stick on his shoulder and headed towards the evil forest. The high priest together with the people of Asase followed him with prayers and tears of sorrow.

THEY ALL STOPPED WHEN Kwaku Ananse reached the threshold of the evil forest. He addressed his people for the last time, saying, 'I have reached the threshold of life and death, the beginning of my journey. Shall my beginning indeed become my end? And shall my first step become my last step? As I have come, so I shall leave you. Alone we have all come, and alone we shall all depart, although I have chosen a shorter path. I have chosen this path so that I shall serve as an example unto you. The more loving you are, the greater the responsibility you must shoulder. I embark on a journey without being certain of my destination.

'THE BRAVE MAN IS ONE who embraces the darkest future. The darkest thing in the world is the future. No one can see what it contains. The courageous man is one who deserves stronger legs. The timid man is one who sits in contemplation of the good things of yesterday. How can there be progress when there is fear of the unknown? Many are the obstacles that await the man who walks the lonely path. I shall surely journey this path, because the seed of the journey I have long since sown in the shrine of our god. Shall the high priest nurture it with tears of my joy or tears of my sorrow? I know not the fruit borne in the womb of time.

'The seed has sprouted from the soil of our god, and this is all I know with certainty as of yet. Whether it shall bear a poisonous fruit or the juice of its fruit shall become nectar unto my body, I know not, for what is certain has passed, belonging to the treasures of yesterday. I am about to harvest the fruit of my own seed in the unknown. If no one enters and comes back alive, who shall report the findings of that which has remained hidden to the people of Asase? The people of Asase will otherwise continue to live in fear and darkness.

'OUR OWN LAND WE FEAR to explore. Who is the foreigner whom we await to shed light on our ignorance? When there is weed in our backyard, do we invite our neighbours to clear it?

'THE TIME HAS COME TO embrace the unknown. I have spent my youth with you. The rest of my life I will spend in pursuit of the unknown that lies hidden in the depth of this great ocean that lies before me. I cannot enter and swim with my clothes on me. Naked I enter. I therefore leave my clothes for your keep, people of Asase. When I sink and never return, let my clothes be unto you the symbol of my love. I am about to sacrifice my body for the greater good of my people. Be united like the individual threads that lost their uniqueness to form my clothes. You shall become more useful than the individual threads that you formerly were.

'I AM AWARE OF THE RISK that awaits me on this journey that I embark on. No one embarks on a journey that the heart is ignorant of. Hidden in each man's heart is the map of his journey. If death is my destination, then so shall it be. For that shall become the final destination of every man born from the womb of the unknown. From the unknown we have come, and to the unknown we shall all return.

'I HAVE TASTED ENOUGH of that which is called life in the land of Asase. I have tasted her food and drunk her water. I have lain with her beautiful daughters at night. Fornicator and sinner I am. I have given alms to Asase's needy palms. Many more things, good and bad, I have done that I do not remember.

'AS NEW LEAVES ARE BORN, so shall old leaves die to make room. Is death not the companion of life in the wheel of progress? How can a tree bear new leaves when old leaves do not give way to new leaves? And how can the tree bear fruit when the new leaves continue to dance an eternal dance in the sunlight without coming to rest in the peaceful bed of death? Even the great sun itself rests in the west after a day's journey from the east. Permit me to say that death and life are the two legs of progress. Each has to be repeated in movement if there is to be forward movement or progress.

'Are my sins going to hunt me now that I decide to leave them behind? What about my good works? Will they come and reward me during my time of need? Will they lead me as my walking stick, or face me from the east as the rising sun in order to brighten the path that is before me? But I cannot face the rising sun without a shadow being cast at my back. Shall I move towards the east and meet the rising sun at midday, or shall I wait in devotion for the light to approach me?

'IF MY PROGRESS IS GOING to be determined by the length of the shadow I cast on the ground, then the middle way entices me with more promise than the earlier two paths. So which of the voices shall I heed?'

THE HIGH PRIEST THEN spoke. 'We cannot give you answers to your numerous questions. We followed you here, but we did not bring you here. Even if we had brought the horse to the river's side, we couldn't have forced it to drink the water. We cannot decide for you. The decision is yours to make. We can only pray for those who choose to tread the path of the brave and the wise. It is not too late to return with us. But when you take the first step into the evil forest, it will be. Ponder deeply before you take the next step, either towards the north or back to the south.

'WHEN YOU MOVE FORWARD, remember not to look back, for that is the sign of indecision, the act of a coward. The dog barks not to attack but to gauge the vulnerability of the intended prey. When you show it courage, it flees. But when you show cowardice, it attacks. Beware! The demons of Asase wait patiently at the door to thy soul, waiting for a sign to enter the door, in order to accompany you on your journey. When you show them fear, they shall happily enter to devour you.

'I HAVE SPOKEN ENOUGH. Now you stand at the threshold of life and death. The next step is yours to take.' Having spoken, the high priest turned back and moved towards the main town, the crowds following him. Kwaku Ananse then took a bold step into the evil forest.

THE FOREST WAS VERY thick with many wild plants. With the aid of a stick Kwaku Ananse found on the ground, he hacked his way through the thick forest. He had started the journey two hours after midday. After continuously walking for a period of five hours, he rested under a neem tree and ate some food and drank some water. He climbed a nearby oil palm tree and brought down some of its branches to prepare a bed. He rested his body, as he was very tired after his long walk.

AFTER KWAKU ANANSE had rested a while, Mens Mentis said to him, 'For how long are we going to travel before we meet this devil, which we know not whether it be man or animal?'

THEN EMOVERE SAID, 'Let's continue the journey before our food runs out.' Kwaku Ananse rose from the palm bed and continued his journey.

AFTER A DAY OF WALKING, when night drew closer, Mens Mentis told Kwaku Ananse, 'We cannot continue walking in the dark. Let's set up a shelter and rest till morning.' Kwaku Ananse saw other oil palm trees. He cut some of the branches and prepared a simple shelter for the night. He ate some pineapples and drank a little water to wash down their juice, grateful to the chief's mother. He tied the remaining food and water in the cloth and lay inside his shelter.

HE HAD A GOOD SLEEP and awoke before sunrise. In the morning, Mens Mentis said to him, 'Why don't we set up a stronger shelter that we can use as our abode till we meet the Devil?' Kwaku Ananse said in his heart that it was a good idea.

THEN EMOVERE SAID TO him, 'Let's prepare the shelter now.'

So Kwaku Ananse began to cut down more branches of the oil palm tree to prepare a stronger shelter. Being skilled in the art of building, he was able to set up a shelter that was pleasing to his own eyes. He was tired after building his shelter, so he ate some of the bananas and drank a little water. He realized that he was running out of food, so Mens Mentis advised him to begin searching for food and water in the evil forest. Kwaku Ananse hid his remaining food in the shelter and began an expedition to seek sustenance.

ON HIS JOURNEY, HE cut down several plants to enable him to trace his way back to his shelter. He hunted east and hunted west, but he could not see any sign of food or water. Thus, he returned back to his shelter dismayed. He was very thirsty and hungry after the hunt for food, so he consumed his last rations. In the night, while Kwaku Ananse was resting in the shelter, Mens Mentis conversed with him, saying, 'Are you going to die of hunger in this forest? Why don't you return to the people of Asase? There is so much food there that you can enjoy. ... No. That would be the act of a coward.'

KWAKU ANANSE SPOKE. 'Or should I return with the lie that I have killed the Devil? They shall demand the head of the Devil as evidence. It shall become a great curse on me and my generations to come should they realize that I had lied to them. Or should I die here and forever be remembered by my people as a hero?' Kwaku Ananse decided in his heart that it is better to die a hero than to live as a coward. 'I refuse to be conquered by this forest. I shall conquer it because I am a conqueror.'

HE DECIDED TO RISE and go for a walk. The moment he stepped out of his shelter, he noticed some movement in a nearby bush. He quickly went inside to get his bow and arrows. He did not wait for the movement to pursue him; he quietly pursued it. Mens Mentis asked him, 'Is this the Devil, or an animal for food?' As Kwaku Ananse was pursuing the movement, he realized that the thing causing the movement was heading towards him. He then hid silently behind a nearby neem tree to wait for the stranger. After some minutes, the stranger emerged as an elephant. The elephant stopped moving, and then carefully approached the tree shielding Kwaku Ananse, as if it has sensed his presence. There was an atmosphere of quietness for some minutes, neither Kwaku Ananse nor the elephant moving. Kwaku Ananse eventually looked behind the tree and realized that the elephant was bleeding at one of its legs. It looked as if it had been attacked by some wild creatures in the forest.

HE CAUTIOUSLY APPROACHED the creature, trying to sense any sign that the animal would attack. The elephant did not make any aggressive move towards him, so he trusted it and touched its head. The elephant replied by closing its eyes as a gesture of friendship and trust. Kwaku Ananse quickly searched for herbs that he could use to treat the wound. Managing to find some herbs, he chewed them up and applied them to the wound. The bleeding stopped soon after he had done so.

THE ELEPHANT PASSED its trunk across Kwaku Ananse's body and ran back into the forest. Kwaku Ananse went back into his shelter to ponder on the origin of the elephant. An hour after it had left, the elephant returned with a huge watermelon in its trunk. It gave the fruit to Kwaku Ananse and quickly left, moving in the direction from whence it came. Kwaku Ananse cut the watermelon into two, ate half, and kept the other half for the evening. An hour later, the elephant returned again with two bunches of bananas, one ripe and the other not. It gave them to Kwaku Ananse and once again headed back in the direction it had come from.

KWAKU ANANSE ATE SOME of the ripe bananas and then entered his shelter to rest. While he rested, Mens Mentis addressed him, asking, 'What would happen should this elephant stop visiting? Why don't you follow it to where it has been harvesting those fruits?' Kwaku Ananse knew in his heart that it was a good idea. He waited for the elephant to return so that he could follow it to where it had been harvesting the fruits. Three days passed, but he did not see any sign of the elephant. He became worried.

WHEN KWAKU ANANSE RAN out of food, he went to an oil palm and took some of its fruits for food. For a period of three days, he relied on the food of the oil palm tree. He used some of the leaves of the tree to prepare a broom, which he used every morning to tidy his new home.

ONE DAY, A STRONG WIND came and blew down his shelter. He became very angry and cursed the wind, saying, 'You shall never have a place to rest. See what you have done to my shelter? Even an ant has a place to lay its head. How much more should a son of man have? Your evil intention I shall surely defeat. For I shall build a beautiful shelter that your envious eyes cannot behold, one that your might cannot overcome.'

HE PREPARED A NEW SHELTER within a period of three days. The new shelter was indeed more beautiful and stronger than the old one.

THE DAY AFTER HE HAD finished constructing his new shelter, he was resting in front of it when he spotted two tigers approaching him. He quickly moved inside his shelter and barred the door. The tigers tried with all their might to bring down his shelter in order to devour him, but all their attempts were futile; the shelter was too strong. They soon returned from whence they came. Kwaku Ananse then thanked the wind that destroyed the old shelter for giving him reason to build a stronger shelter.

A WEEK LATER, A VERY heavy rain poured down, flooding the entire vicinity of Kwaku Ananse's shelter. He cursed the rain, saying, 'You shall never have a place to rest. See what you have done to my shelter? Even an ant has a place to lay its head. How much more should a son of man have? Your evil intention I shall surely defeat. I am going to build a more beautiful shelter that your envious eyes cannot behold, one beyond even your reach.'

HE CARRIED HIS BELONGINGS from the shelter and went in search of a hill or mountain. Within hours he found a hill, which he climbed. For a period of three days, he set up a new shelter. During a subsequent seven-day period on the hill, he continued visiting the palm oil tree to eat its fruit and the food contained within its seed. When the fruit was gone from the tree, he called it useless, felled it to ground, and dug a hole in it to extract the sap, which he intended to use for fermented palm wine. He put a calabash under the hole to collect the sap.

HE WENT TO HIS SHELTER and decided to give the palm sap time to ferment, wanting to enjoy an alcohol-rich palm wine. When the day came for him to go and retrieve his palm wine from under the palm tree, he set out on the trek. On his way, he saw two gnomes sitting on a log. These two gnomes were Ingratus and Memor. They invited Kwaku Ananse to come and drink with them. Kwaku Ananse responded that he was a religious man and thus eschewed alcohol. They then asked him whether he was the one who had felled the palm tree. He responded that he knew not the palm tree they were talking about. Kwaku Ananse then asked them why they were concerned about the palm tree that they were talking about. Ingratus and Memor told him that the fallen palm tree used to be their habitat. When the three finished their brief conversation, Kwaku Ananse continued his journey to the fallen palm tree and drank all the palm wine collected in his calabash. He changed his direction home because he didn't want to meet Ingratus and Memor on the way.

TO HIS SURPRISE, HE met them, seated as before, on his new route. He was drunk and had been happily singing and dancing when they saw him. Memor asked him why he was so happy. He said to him that he had taken palm wine from a useless tree he had felled. Memor asked him why he had lied about abstaining from alcohol. He never answered, but continued dancing and singing. Then Ingratus asked him why he called the palm tree useless after it had given him food in the forest. He never answered him but continued dancing. Ingratus and Memor took a stone between them and threw it to hit Kwaku Ananse's ankle. Crying out loud as the two scuttled off into the bushes, he asked, 'What have I done that these little men punish me so hard?'

ON HIS ELEVENTH DAY on the hill, Kwaku Ananse decided to rest in front of his shelter. He scanned as far as he could see from the vantage point of his hill. At noon, he noticed a bright light in the northern part of the forest. Because he had made up his mind not to journey that day, he didn't make any attempt to investigate that which caused the brightness in the evil forest.

WHEN NIGHT CAME, HE had a dream. In his dream, he saw himself on a farm where he was harvesting crops. After the harvest, he prepared some food and ate it. He then found himself at his home in Asase. He tried to open the door to his room but realized that he didn't have the key to do so. He therefore sat under a mango tree to rest. While he was resting, a man and a little girl approached him and asked him why he was sitting under the mango tree. He told them he could not find the key to his room. The man gave him a key, and the little girl also gave him a key. After taking the keys from the two people, who were personally known to him in his community in Asase as Helios and Perse respectively, he went to the door to try the keys. When he reached the entrance, the two keys in his hand became one. He inserted the key into the keyhole and opened the door. In the dream, he went inside and was about to sleep on his bed when he awoke from sleep.

JUST THEN, MENS MENTIS asked him, 'What message did these two people seek to deliver? Helios is a carpenter in Asase, and Perse is that little girl who was born recently to the baker. You don't have any special relationship with these two people. Why, then, do you dream about them? What do these two people have in common that they appear in your dream? If the key represents a solution, what wisdom do these two people have that surpasses the wisdom of Kwaku Ananse?'

KWAKU ANANSE ROSE UP from his bed after listening to the silent speech of Mens Mentis. It was morning and Kwaku Ananse was very hungry. He stood in front of his house to see if he could behold the brightness he had seen the other day, but it had gone. He waited until it was noon, at which time he went to stand there again to see whether he could behold the light. To his surprise, he saw the radiation again. He therefore descended the hill and headed in the direction of the light. Upon reaching the location, he found no light, only a freshwater swamp forest. He became happy when he found water in the evil forest, because he was very thirsty. He bowed down and drank some of the water. Thereafter he thanked the rain that had forced him to relocate to the top of the hill.

AS SOON AS HE FINISHED thanking the rain and was about to leave, he saw a swarm of bees coming to attack him. He dived into the swamp and swam until he reached the other side of the swamp forest.

TO HIS AMAZEMENT, HE saw a very beautiful garden just beyond the swamp, with all kinds of beautiful trees. The garden was blessed with all kinds of fruits, such as berries, mangoes, apples, bananas, and pineapples. The entire floor of the garden was covered with beautiful flowers: hypericum, berry, gloriosa lily, anemone, anthurium, mokara orchids, gladiolus, ranunculus, peony, ginger, alstroemeria, gerbera daisy, carnation, and rose.

WHEN HE SAW THE BEAUTY, variety, and quantity of the fruits, he took more than he could eat. When he had finished eating, he plucked as many as he could and tied them in a cloth. On his way home, he saw two gnomes sitting on a log. Kwaku Ananse greeted them. Once they responded, he asked, 'Have you come to punish me like you did the other time?'

ONE OF THEM REPLIED, 'My brother is Avaritia, and I am Liberalitas. We don't remember ever teaching you in this forest.'

KWAKU ANANSE SAID, 'Sorry then. You look like some little men I once met.'

AVARITIA ASKED KWAKU Ananse to give him some of his fruit. Kwaku Ananse told him that the fruits belonged to him and his family, so there wasn't enough to share with them. Avaritia asked him where his wife and children lived. Kwaku Ananse pointed to the top of the hill and told Avaritia that they lived with him there. Liberalitas asked him to extend his regards to his wife and children. Kwaku Ananse promised to deliver the message. He wished them goodbye and headed home.

WHEN KWAKU ANANSE REACHED home and was about to eat the fruits, the gnomes appeared before him and greeted him. They told him that they had come to personally say hello to his wife and children because they had never spotted them in the forest. Kwaku Ananse told them his wife and children had gone out to fetch water. The gnomes left, only to come back later. Upon their return, they realized that Kwaku Ananse had eaten most of the fruits and was about to eat the last one.

THEY ASKED HIM WHY he had lied to them when he told them that the fruits were for him and his family, and he said it was because the fruits were too beautiful to share with others. Liberalitas, who had a rod in his hand, gave him twenty-one lashes and advised him to be generous. Early in the morning, Kwaku Ananse realized that he was very sick. As a result, he couldn't go out the whole day. He vomited and felt very cold. Mens Mentis told him, 'You have allowed greed to override your conscience. See how you are suffering?'

AFTER THAT DAY, KWAKU Ananse experienced a comfortable stay in the garden for a period of one month. One day, on his way home after gathering fruits and nuts in the garden beyond the swamp, lightning struck his shelter on the hill. The entire shelter caught fire and burned to ashes. When he saw what the lightning had done to his shelter, he cursed the lightning, saying, 'Where do you expect a son of man to lay his head? Even the ant has a place to sleep. May the curse of Asase god come on you. Shame on you! Your evil purpose I shall defeat. I shall set up a new shelter near the water in the garden that your envious eyes cannot behold. And when you strike it again, I shall have enough water to put your fire out.'

NOW THAT HE HAD NOTHING to call his belongings except his cutlass, he went to find a location to set up a new shelter close to the swamp. He said in his heart, I shall set up a new shelter in this garden, and it shall become my final place of abode in this forest.

HE STOOD AT A PLACE in the garden that he considered to be an appropriate spot for him to set up his garden. He scanned through the garden to see if he could find a good tree to use for his new shelter. A certain tree in the middle of the garden came to his attention. The tree had three branches, he found a reptilian being in the spot where the three branches met. The snake man was in deep sleep and did not show any sign of life. Kwaku Ananse used his sword to touch the snake man in order to wake it. The instant he touched the snake man with the cutlass, he raised its head and asked, 'Why have you awakened me from my slumber, sir?'

KWAKU ANANSE REPLIED, 'I have come to kill you, speaking snake. Your ability to speak suggests to me that you are not an ordinary snake, but the very Devil in this evil forest that I have travelled far to slay.'

THE SNAKE MAN ASKED Kwaku Ananse, "Why do you call this forest evil when it has fed you and sheltered you?'

KWAKU ANANSE REPLIED, 'I call this forest evil because it is the abode of you, the speaking snake. I am in a hurry to carry the good news to my people. Say your last words before I slay you with the cutlass I hold in my hand.'

The snake man said to Kwaku Ananse, 'A very old serpent I am. Long have I waited to be killed by a son of man. Before you slay me with your cutlass, give me the opportunity to sing a song to this garden, which has accommodated me for a long period of time.'

Kwaku Ananse said, 'Sing your last song before I slay you with this cutlass.'

The snake began singing the following lyrics:

Onufu is my name.

The ancient ones honoured me as the bringer of knowledge and immortality,

Because I gave them the soma of the gods and journeyed with them through the god lands.

From the south they came.

To the north we went, till they became ubiquitous at the end of their journey.

Now I have fallen from my place of honour and have become a symbol of evil.

The place of my abode is now called the forbidden forest.

I sing my last song to this garden.

This is my last song, for the son of man is about to slay me with his cutlass.

I die in peace with my secret knowledge of wisdom and immortality.

AFTER HEARING THE SONG of Onufu, Ananse said 'I'm not trying to be mean, I'm just being frank with you. Your voice sounds so horrible, devil. I wasn't impressed with your song at all.'

'I'm not offended don't worry, the cat is never impressed no matter how well a mouse dances, Onufu replied. Ananse then thought in his heart, 'why don't I take the devil to the god lands to find out whether that which he talks about in his song is true? He then asked Onufu, 'where are these god lands that you sang about? Onufu answered: With fire Ice can be changed from visible to invincible.

'I'm in a hurry to deliver your head to my people so let's execute this mission quickly.' Ananse said.

The reptoid being pulled a certain rod with a flame at the edge, touching Kwaku Ananse with the rod, they both vanished and appeared in a tunnel.

He then shouted from inside it with a very deep voice, 'Follow me. Let's journey to the god lands.'

They journeyed through the tunnel for seven hours, and then they came to an opening filled with water.

Chapter Three

The Test and Trial in Ewiase

A CROCODILE APPEARED from the water and prostrated itself before Kwaku Ananse. Onufu asked Kwaku Ananse to mount the crocodile, and he did so. Onufu wrapped his body around the tail of the crocodile, and the crocodile carried them on the surface of the water. While on the crocodile, Onufu gave Kwaku Ananse the names of all the god lands that were before them. They travelled for hours, eventually reaching the city of Ewiase, which was encircled by water. The crocodile took them to one of the six entrances leading into the inner city of Ewiase. The people of Ewiase considered the waters of Ewiase to be part of their city, as they held several recreational activities on the water during their major festivals.

There were men guarding the entrances to the city of Ewiase. Kwaku Ananse came face-to-face with one of the guardians, who asked him why he wanted to enter the city. He replied that he wanted to transit across the city of Ewiase to the next city of Tumikrom. The guardian asked him whether he could speak the language of the Ewiasians. He answered no.

Then the guardian told him that before he could transit through to the next city of Tumikrom, he would have to eat the ambrosia and drink the nectar of the god of Ewiase. He added that the ambrosia and nectar is only given to those who understand the language of the Ewiasians.

At this point, Onufu spoke. 'We have travelled very far from the city of Asase, so kindly give him the chance to stay a while in this city to learn the language of the people of Ewiase.'

The guardian asked Kwaku Ananse, 'Are you willing to stay in the city of Ewiase to exercise the patience and undergo the sacrifice required to learn her language?'

Kwaku Ananse responded, 'Yes, I am ready to exercise the patience and undergo the sacrifice it takes to learn the language of Ewiase.'

'Then you are granted entry into the water city of Ewiase.' Kwaku Ananse and Onufu thanked the guardian and entered Ewiase.

Onufu had a perfect knowledge of every sector of the city, as if he were one of the inhabitants. He took Kwaku Ananse to the king's palace.

When they reached the palace, Kwaku Ananse was given a seat and was soon given water to drink. The king inquired of Kwaku Ananse as to his reason for coming to the palace. Kwaku Ananse responded that he had come to learn the language of the people of Ewiase in order to eat the ambrosia and drink the nectar of the god of Ewiase. The king then invited the elders of Ewiase into the palace to inform them of Kwaku Ananse's decision to learn their language. He requested for one person to volunteer to teach Kwaku Ananse the language of Ewiase. One elder by the name Mundus volunteered to perform the task. The king then asked Kwaku Ananse to excuse them as they conferred to reach an agreement on how the training would be conducted. Kwaku Ananse excused the king and his elders, including the one who was known by the name Mundus.

The king then asked Mundus to teach Kwaku Ananse the language of Ewiase for a period of three months. After those three months, Kwaku Ananse would be free, and eligible to be given the ambrosia and nectar of the god of Ewiase. Hearing this, Onufu approached the group and entreated Mundus to release Kwaku Ananse after three months. Mundus replied, 'After three months, I shall release him when he voluntarily decides to leave. If he decides to stay after the third month, then I shall continue to keep him in my home. He who decides to forsake the pleasures of my garden in order to continue his journey is one who has perfectly learnt the language of Ewiase. So unless he expresses his volition to leave, I shall continue to keep him in my garden.'

The king then asked Mundus, 'What role shall the snake play during the training period?'

Mundus answered, 'The snake shall remain silent till Kwaku Ananse expresses his own desire to leave my garden. I shall keep the snake on top of the Iboga tree planted in the garden.'

Then Onufu spoke. 'That is not a fair agreement. I shall desist from talking to him or reminding him of what is ahead of him unless he eats the root bark of the iboga tree. I shall be grateful if that is also included in the agreement.'

The king asked Mundus and the snake, 'Have we been able to reach an agreement yet?'

Mundus replied, 'I shall agree to his request. However, I shall make the Iboga tree on which the snake abides a forbidden one, so that Kwaku Ananse will have no opportunity to talk to the snake.' Onufu agreed to the proposal, and they sealed the agreement.

Now that the parties had reached a consensus, Kwaku Ananse was invited inside the palace and handed over to Mundus. Mundus took Kwaku Ananse and Onufu to his home. When they arrived, Onufu entered the garden and climbed the Iboga tree as agreed.

Mundus, who had a very beautiful home in Ewiase, introduced Kwaku Ananse to all the animals in the garden on the first day. He also introduced him to all the plants in the garden. The garden was filled with all the fruits and herbs in the world. He advised Kwaku Ananse to eat all the plants in the garden except the Iboga tree in the middle of the garden. Kwaku Ananse asked why he was not to eat the Iboga in the garden. Mundus replied that the day he ate the root bark of the iboga tree, he would die. He also told him not to work, because the garden would meet all his needs.

Kwaku Ananse, when he wasn't studying the language, spent most of his time playing with the dolphins in a body of water in the midst of the garden. All the animals were friendly with him. One particular animal that he developed special friendly ties with was a chimpanzee. Sometimes he had a very great desire to communicate with his pet friends in the garden, but whenever he tried, it was in vain.

One day he went to Mundus and said to him, 'The companions that you gave me are very friendly and beautiful beings. The only problem I have is their failure to understand me. I wish they could also talk like the way I talk, and think the way I think.'

Mundus said to him, 'I understand what your real needs are. I promised you the very day you came to this garden that I would do anything to make your stay here comfortable. I will bring you a woman who is much like you. She will make you happy all the time, for life in this garden would be painful to undergo without a partner. When she comes, all your sorrows will be wiped away.'

Kwaku Ananse became very excited, and yearned for her in his heart. He asked Mundus, 'So when are you going to bring me this woman that you talk about?'

Mundus answered, 'I shall bring her tomorrow.'

But by the end of the next day, Kwaku Ananse had not seen any woman, so he went to Mundus to ask him about her. 'You promised to bring the woman today, but the day is almost over.'

'She is on her way,' Mundus replied. 'Have patience another day and you shall see her face.'

The next day passed and Kwaku Ananse did not see the face of the woman, so he went to Mundus and asked him, 'Why is the woman not here yet? The sound of her footsteps echoes in my heart.'

Mundus answered, 'She is crossing a great ocean to reach you. The path that she has to cross in order to reach you is not a pleasant one. It is one full of calamities and suffering. But she shall surely be here tomorrow.'

The following day, the woman arrived in Mundus's garden. Mundus introduced her to Kwaku Ananse and said to him, 'This one is really one with you. So you shall call her Aso, because she is the bone of your bone and the flesh of your flesh. She will help eliminate all your sufferings and replace them with joy. You cannot live without her.'

Kwaku Ananse became very excited when he heard those promises from Mundus. He took Aso by the hand and toured the entire garden with her. She became very happy once she saw the beautiful natural scenes. Kwaku Ananse told her she could touch every fruit in the garden except the one in the middle of the garden, which was forbidden.

The two of them did everything together in the garden. They swam the waters together and climbed the trees together. They walked together and ran together. They smiled together and laughed together. If there would have been sorrow in the garden, they would have shed tears together, but there was nothing like that in the garden.

One day when Ananse was asleep, Asor decided to visit the main town of Ewiase. There, she met a sick gentleman called Invidia. Asor felt pity for Invidia, so she secretly slipped out of the garden to see him each night as Ananse slept to give him healing. One day, Ananse woke up from sleep in the middle of the night, and Asor was nowhere to be found. He searched the garden but could not see her. He became very troubled at heart. Nevertheless, he went back to lie down in sleep.

The following morning, when he asked Aso where she had been during the night, she failed to give him a convincing answer, so he warned her that he was not going to allow her to have her freedom from that day on.

By this time, a year had passed since the day Kwaku Ananse had come to the garden of Mundus. He had forgotten the reason that brought him to the land of Ewiase, as Aso had become his whole reason for being there.

When Invidia realized that Aso wasn't going to come to him again, he started to present her with gifts in Mundus's garden.

One day, when Aso was relaxing in her room, Invidia came to the house and met Kwaku Ananse, who was sitting in front of the door. He greeted Kwaku Ananse and said, 'I have come to present this gift of a flower to a woman here by the name of Aso.'

Kwaku Ananse collected the flower and said, 'I shall deliver it to her.'

When Invidia had left, Emovere said to Kwaku Ananse, 'When you make the mistake to present this flower to Aso, she will be enchanted by it and love Invidia, who wants to snatch your source of happiness from you. Destroy the flower and get Aso a better flower, one that will be more pleasing to her eyes.' Kwaku Ananse destroyed the flower and went into the garden to pick a different flower, which he then presented to Aso, saying, 'A certain gentleman by the name Invidia was here to present a withered flower as a gift to you. I destroyed it and brought you this beautiful one, which I consider to be more fitting as a gift to a goddess.' Aso accepted the flower, although she wasn't happy about the whole story relating to it.

The next day, Invidia came again and presented another flower. Again, Kwaku Ananse destroyed it and presented Aso with a different one

The following day, a different man, called Ira, visited the garden of Mundus to look for Aso. When Kwaku Ananse heard that he was looking for Aso, he pounced on Ira and fought with him.

Aso became deeply unhappy with Kwaku Ananse, so she went to sit under the forbidden tree to cry. While sitting under the forbidden tree, she heard a voice. It was the voice of Onufu. 'Why are you crying, my lady?'

Aso answered, 'My companion in this garden is not letting me have my freedom. He doesn't want me to have any other friend apart from him. His attention has now been shifted to Ira after Invidia, and that saddens my heart. I have become fed up with life in this garden of Mundus, so I desire to leave it, but Mundus will not allow me to leave Kwaku Ananse alone here.'

Onufu told her that Mundus would only allow her to leave the garden when Kwaku Ananse decided to leave. Aso replied, 'Kwaku Ananse is so much in love with this garden and would not leave it for any reason.' Onufu then related to Aso the reason why Kwaku Ananse had first come to the city of Ewiase. Aso then asked Onufu, 'So how can we help him to recover that forgotten memory?'

'That which he clings to in this garden is vanity. So when we uncover the nakedness of the vanity before his eyes, he will be prompted to remembrance,' answered Onufu.

Aso asked, 'But how can we uncover the nakedness of vanity before his eyes?'

'Give him the root bark of the iboga tree to eat, and then he shall realize the vanity of that which has erased his memory,' Onufu replied.

Aso objected. 'But Mundus has told us that we shouldn't eat the iboga because it is forbidden.'

'Mundus's desire is to keep Kwaku Ananse in this garden forever. Through toil, a man grows. See how Mundus has made everything sweet in this garden for Kwaku Ananse? He doesn't understand what suffering means. He only knows joy and happiness. Let Kwaku Ananse leave this garden, and then he shall grow to become the ubiquitous sapien that his father is. This iboga will not let him die as Mundus proclaims. It shall rather let him distinguish between what is good and what is evil. And this knowledge will guide him to become the ubiquitous sapien that his true heart hopes to become. Taste it and see whether you will really die.'

Aso was convinced by Onufu, so she tasted the iboga. She realized that it was sweet. After she tasted the iboga, Onufu asked her, 'What do you feel? Have you died?'

'It is very sweet, speaking snake. How can I convince Kwaku Ananse to follow me to this place to eat the iboga? Why don't you give me one to present to him in the house?'

'I desire to speak to him also,' said Onufu, 'so bring him here, and then you shall have your freedom from the garden of Mundus. You have all it takes to bring him here. Your charm was not given unto you to please his selfish desires but to help him grow. If you cannot use your charm to bring him to the forbidden tree, then what is the essence of your power, woman?' Aso agreed to bring Kwaku Ananse to the forbidden tree to eat the iboga root bark.

The following morning, Aso asked Kwaku Ananse to accompany her to the forbidden tree. But Kwaku Ananse insisted that he would not defy the orders given to him by his master, Mundus. Aso uncovered her legs before Kwaku Ananse and asked him, 'Do you want these to be yours forever?'

Kwaku Ananse replied, 'Yes, I want them to be mine forever.'

Aso said, 'Then follow me, and they shall become yours.'

Kwaku Ananse followed Aso to the forbidden tree. When they were a third of the way there, Kwaku Ananse said, 'I have changed my mind. I am not moving any further.'

ASO THEN UNCOVERED her upper body before him and asked him of her breasts, 'Do you want these to be yours forever?'

Kwaku Ananse replied, 'Yes, I want them to be mine forever.'

Aso said, 'Then follow me, and they shall be yours forever.' Kwaku Ananse followed her because he was so much in love with that which he saw with his eyes.

When they had passed two-thirds of the distance, Kwaku Ananse stopped and said, 'I am not moving any further.'

Aso kissed him and asked him, 'Do you like the lips that you just kissed?'

Kwaku Ananse answered, 'Yes, and I desire to have them for myself forever and ever.'

Aso said, 'Then follow me.' Kwaku Ananse duly followed her until they reached the forbidden tree. When they arrived, Aso uncovered her whole body before Kwaku Ananse and asked him, 'Are you now ready to eat?'

Kwaku Ananse replied without hesitating. 'I am ready, my love.'

Aso gave him some iboga root bark to eat. When he had eaten half of the root bark, Aso asked him, 'Are you enjoying it?'

'I am enjoying it but it taste very awful.' When he finished eating it, he was satisfied.

Aso then asked him if he wanted another. Kwaku Ananse replied, 'I am satisfied and desire no more.'

Ananse vomited many unclean substances in his body and laid down on a bed of leaves for 24 hours.

A gentleman who identified himself as Mr iboga appeared before in his vision and reminded him about his mission in Ewiase. He cried out loud and said, 'Mundus has deceived me. To what end is the sweetness in this garden? To what end is the sweetness of this lady whom he boasted about? See how long I have spent in this garden clinging unto vanities! I shall leave today.'

Kwaku Ananse went to Mundus and informed him of his decision to continue his journey to Tumikrom. Mundus became very angry when Kwaku Ananse told him that he was going to leave. He asked him, 'Did you eat the forbidden tree?'

Kwaku Ananse answered, 'It was that woman you brought me who gave me the tree to eat.'

MUNDUS CONSENTED TO Kwaku Ananse and Aso, together with Onufu, leaving his garden, as he had promised.

The great feast of the god of Ewiase was celebrated in honour of Kwaku Ananse's and Aso's victory over emotional attachment, for that had been the test in the garden. The high priest said to them, 'You have just eaten the Soma of the god of Ewiase. Henceforth, you shall become impervious to water. Therefore, no water can cause you harm.'

They were given a place to sleep in the palace that night.

Chapter Four

The Asase Yaa Mission

WHEN MORNING CAME, Kwaku Ananse and Aso, together with Onufu, set out on their journey to the land of Tumikrom. The people of Ewiase bade them farewell, playing music from harps and trumpets as their custom demanded. As the party got to the banks of the water that surrounded the city of Ewiase, two crocodiles appeared from the water to carry the three travellers on their backs. They crossed the body of water that led to a faraway land to the north of Ewiase, the land of Tumikrom.

They arrived at the city of Tumikrom in the afternoon. The entire city was surrounded by a triangular wall with ten entrances. When they approached one of the entrances leading to the inner city of Tumikrom, they saw a guardian, who greeted them. 'Welcome back home, our lady Aso, queen of the great city of Tumikrom. You are also welcome, Kwaku Ananse, the twin soul of the queen of Tumikrom. My lady, may I know why your twin soul seeks entry into this great city?'

'He has passed the test of attachment and therefore seeks entry in order to undergo the test and trial of Tumikrom,' she replied.

The guardian then said to Kwaku Ananse, 'Good gentleman! Are you ready to pass through the terror of fire and also to unveil your inner fire to the eyes of the inhabitants of Tumikrom for examination?'

'Yes, guardian, I am ready to do as required by the goddess and people of Tumikrom City,' Kwaku Ananse answered.

'Then remember to keep your inner flame in check if you really want to behold the sight of the Aerocorn of Tumikrom. I grant you entry into the city of Tumikrom.' Kwaku Ananse and Aso thanked him, and then they entered the inner city. Seeing two white horses awaiting them beyond the gate, they mounted the horses and rode deeper into the inner city of Tumikrom. When the people of Tumikrom beheld their queen and her twin soul riding the horses, they shouted with joy. They assembled a variety of musical instruments and played lovely tunes to welcome back their queen after her long absence from Tumikrom.

The city of Tumikrom had scores of beautiful trees and several waterfalls. The entire ground of the city was covered with leopard's bane, wild licorice, agrimony, and moschatel.

After the celebration of the return of Tumikrom's queen, Kwaku Ananse was taken to the palace of Tumikrom, where Aso had her throne.

There were two thrones in the palace of Tumikrom. Kwaku Ananse sat on the right one and Aso sat on the left. Kwaku Ananse then said, 'I never knew you were a queen, my lady. What a beautiful palace you have. What reason inspired you to temporarily abandon your beautiful palace to come to the house of Mundus?'

'The reason that brought me to the house of Mundus was you, Kwaku Ananse,' she answered.

'What reason prompted you to pursue me in the house of Mundus, my lady?'

'My heart sought love and union.' Asor answered.

'And why did you cheat with Inivia and Ira if I was your main reason for visiting the garden?

'I never cheated with Invidia and Ira. They were both sick and I had to give them healing before I could attain the union that my heart sought. Let me further explain.'Asor then narrated a tale to Ananse.

'There lived a man called Dominos Domino. He had very fertile soil but had no plants in it. Also, he had a slave by the name Hermaphroditus. He one day called Hermaphroditus to him. "I am very hungry because there is no plant to provide food on this fertile land that I possess. I want you to travel to the faraway land of Asase. There is a tree called the bonum et malum tree. It is so called because of its two fruits, called bonum and malum. I want you to bring me seven hundred bonum fruits. I shall eat them and sow the seed in our fertile land.

'"When you get to the land of Asase, you may be given many seeds to choose from. Remember to choose a good seed that will bear very sweet fruit. Cultivate there a tree, and return to me with the fruit it bears. Make sure you bring as many fruits as you can, because the distance from here to Asase is very long. It would take you a period of nine months for you to tread."

'Hermaphroditus embarked on the journey that spanned a period of nine months. When he got to Asase, he was directed to a certain gardener who gave him several seeds of the bonum et malum plant to choose from. The seeds had different colours, so he chose his favourite colour from the proffered selection. The gardener gave him land to sow the seed and also water to nurture it.

'Through toil and pain, he was able to nurture the seed to become a bonum et malum tree. He plucked four of the fruits, as his hand was large enough to carry only two of each. He travelled back to the land of his master and presented the fruits to him. Dominos Domino tasted the fruits and spoke. "I told you to bring me only sweet fruits. How come you brought two sweet ones and two sour ones?

'"I shall sow the seeds of the sweeter ones in my soil. Take back the seeds of the sour ones to Asase, and sow them and nurture them to bear sweeter fruits." Hermaphroditus begged Dominos Domino to allow him to rest a while before embarking on another journey. Yet Dominos Domino replied, "You know the distance from here to Asase is very long and not easy to cross. Why didn't you work harder to bring only bonum fruits? Out of your laziness, you decided to bring two bonum fruits and two malum fruits, the latter of which you know I dislike. How can only two bonum fruits satisfy me? I am granting you a rest period of two months. After that period, you will have to go back to Asase to transform those seeds into bonum fruits."

'After the two-month rest period, Hermaphroditus embarked on his second journey to transform the malum seeds into bonum fruits. When he reached Asase, he begged the gardener to give him another piece of land to transform the malum seeds into bonum fruits. He was offered land, and so he planted the malum seed and nurtured it with his sweat and toil. When it became a tree with fruits, he plucked four of the fruits and travelled to the land of Dominos Domino to present them to his master.

'When Dominos Domino tasted the four fruits, he found that three of them were malum and only one was bonum. He became very angry and said to Hermaphroditus, "You know the bonum et malum fruit in Asase contains a seed, but when these seeds are sown in our land, the fruits they bear contain no seed. For how long would I have to wait to fill this fertile soil of mine with bonum trees? You should also be aware that even the first two bonum seeds you gave me have not fully matured.

"'I am allergic to malum fruits. Why did you travel all the way from here to Asase to bring me three malum fruits and one bonum fruit? Even with four bonum fruits, I am not full. Why do you stubbornly starve your master?

"'I shall give you a helper who will help you accomplish the mission that I have assigned thee. I shall divide you into two, so that when you bring four, your helper shall also bring four, till I sow the seven hundred bonum seeds in my land. Together, you shall bring eight in a season, which may satisfy me yet."

'In the evening while Hermaphroditus was asleep, Dominos Domino removed one of his ribs, out of which he created another human, whom he named Femina. He breathed some of his vital essence into her to give her life, just like he had done when he created Hermaphroditus. He then changed the name of Hermaphroditus to Vir, because the creation of Femina caused some of the inner and outer features of Hermaphroditus to change. He asked Femina to go first while Vir helped him with the farm work.

'Femina went to Asase. On her first attempt, she brought three bonum fruits and one malum fruit. When she returned, Vir was asked to go while Femina rested and helped Dominos Domino on the farm. He returned with two bonum and two malum fruits.

'Sometimes they went together, and other times one went while the other stayed behind. Finally, Femina was able to complete her assignment before Vir. She therefore volunteered to help Vir complete his assignment. Vir could not complete his assignment in time because he had allowed unnecessary attachments to things and people in Asase to distract him from concentrating on his mission.

'When Femina joined him in Asase to help him complete his mission, he tried to attach himself to her. But Femina, being more experienced, and knowing the mission that brought her to Asase, refused to dance to the tune of vanities with Vir.

'Vir became hurt when Femina refused to dance with him. Out of the pain he suffered, he meditated on the cause of his suffering, and as a result he gained liberation from his attachment to vanities. That enabled Vir to complete his mission, and the two of them were then able to return home.'

Kwaku Ananse smiled. 'Thanks so much for clarifying the beautiful story of our yesterday. Now, tell me about that which is in the womb and is about to be delivered.'

Aso instructed that a man by the name Auctoritas be brought before them in the palace. Aso then told Kwaku Ananse, 'A new temple is to be built for the goddess of Asase . I present to you Auctoritas, who shall become the supervisor of the work. You shall become his master. Kwaku Ananse, my love, please promise me that you shall build a very beautiful temple for Asase Yaa.'

'It is a great honour to be given such an opportunity. I shall execute your assignment to your greatest satisfaction, my lady,' he replied.

Aso then said, 'When you are able to accomplish thy assignment
with perfection, we shall be granted access to the city of Odokrom by
the Aerocorn of Tumikrom. It is night now. I wish to retire to my bed.
Visit me in my inner chamber and let's make love till morning, whereby
your inner fire will be activated for you to commence thy assignment.' He
willingly did as she required, because his greatest desire was to become
one with the bone of his bone and the flesh of his own flesh.

The next morning, Kwaku Ananse was taken to the site where the
construction of the temple was to be done. Thirty Tumikromians
volunteered to help build the temple of their goddess . The plan of the
temple was given to Kwaku Ananse to study. After studying the plan, he
inspected the site and made a request for the necessary materials.

The next morning, Kwaku Ananse began giving orders for the
construction of the temple through Auctoritas. For a period of six
months, he constructed the temple of Asase Yaa.After the completion of
the temple, he reported to Aso that he had finished, and so Aso came to
inspect it. When Aso got to the site of the new temple, the entire temple
collapsed to the ground.

'How come the entire temple has collapsed before me? Asase Yaa is
not satisfied with thy work.'

'Aso, my lady, blame Auctoritas for the failure. He had low energy
and a weaker will. He also had fear of some of the volunteers, so he could
not instruct them with confidence,' Kwaku Ananse responded.

Aso said, 'O Kwaku Ananse! Why did you allow Auctoritas to have
those deficiencies? It was thy responsibility to have granted him the
confidence that he required to complete thy assignment to perfection.'

'Then give me another chance and I'll fix Auctoritas,' Kwaku Ananse
begged.

'I grant you another opportunity, Kwaku Ananse.'

After another period of six months, Kwaku Ananse reported to Aso
that he had completed the assignment. Aso then went to inspect what

Kwaku Ananse had done. When Aso arrived at the site of the new temple, the entire temple collapsed to the ground.

Aso asked, 'How come the entire temple has collapsed before me yet again? Asase is not satisfied with thy work.'

Kwaku Ananse replied thusly: 'Aso, my lady, blame Auctoritas for the failure. He had excessive energy and was overly aggressive. He over-controlled and was manipulative to boot!'

Aso responded, 'O Kwaku Ananse! Why did you allow Auctoritas to have that excessive and selfish energy?'

Kwaku Ananse begged again: 'Give me another chance to fix Auctoritas.'

'I grant you another opportunity, Kwaku Ananse.'

After yet another period of six months, Kwaku Ananse reported to Aso that he had completed the assignment. Aso then went to inspect what Kwaku Ananse had done. This time around, the temple stood strong and was sound.

'How were you able to build such a magnificent temple?' Aso asked.

'Through respect for the emotions of the volunteers and a feeling of unity with them; through inner harmony, a feeling of tranquillity, and a sense of humour; and also through confidence have I completed the task,' he replied.

Aso said, 'Congratulations for passing the test of Auctoritas. I passed this test long ago, and patiently have I waited for you to complete yours, as it has enabled us to fly with the Aerocorn of Tumikrom.'

The next day, Aso presented the palace to the Tumikromian people and said to them, 'People of Tumikrom, we have completed the test that you gave us. Let this Cathedral be named after the goddess of Asase, Asase Yaa.

'Let the Mission of this temple become the Mission of the New Age, and let this Mission be called the Asase Yaa Mission. Asase Yaa Mission shall become the name of this temple and your mother who gives you food to eat, water to drink, clothes to wear, a place to sleep ,herbs to heal your body, teacher plants to heal your soul and everything you need shall be glad that you have shown your appreciation and honoured her. In her excitement, the soil shall become rich, food and water shall become abundant, your herbs shall become potent, the plants shall grow on every part of your land and they shall give healing to your future generations. Your future generations shall be called wise and not believers because they will not believe everything given to them in the name of God.

'The Mission is to empower the people of Tumikrom to take Tumi from the false teachers who teach the people to worship false gods born from the womb of ancient mythologies, which the Sumerian Epic of Gilgamesh and the Akkadian Epic of Atrahasis exposes.

'The Mission is to empower the people of Tumikrom to hold their leaders accountable and to demand transparency in the revenue generated from the natural resources.

'The Mission is to ensure that a hundred percent of all natural resources are benefited by the people.

'LET ALL REVENUE GENERATED from the land be used for the betterment of the people.This is the spirit of the Asase Yaa Mission.

'The Mission is to promote New Age Globalism as against Nationalism.

'The Mission is to inform the leaders that the time has come for them to become the servants and for the people to become the leaders. The time has come for the majority to become the owners.

'The Mission is to remind the majority that they will continue to become slaves and the few will continue to be Kings, when they fail to take the Tumi from the few.

'The Mission is to inform tax payers of Countries with nuclear weapons that the time has come for them to stop funding nuclear programs. The time has come for their leaders to shutdown the nuclear facilities they funded.

'The Mission is to remind those nations with nuclear weapons that they are not great but foolish.

'The Mission is all about life, prosperity, truth, love, peace, unity and equality.

'The people of Tumikrom, we humbly demand that you allow us to mount the Aerocorn and thence travel to the city of Odokrom.'

The people spoke with one voice and said, 'You have passed the test of Asase, water, and fire. Thus, you are no longer ordinary humans but god-men. How can we hold you from mounting the Aerocorn of Tumikrom? The Aerocorn resides in Tumikrom but is the property of the god-men. You may progress on your journey to the land of the god-men.'

They escorted Kwaku Ananse and Aso, together with Onufu, to the base of the tallest mountain in Tumikrom. On top of the mountain stood a winged unicorn, which was referred to as the Aerocorn by the people of Tumikrom.

When Aso, Kwaku Ananse, and Onufu were about to climb the mountain, Mens Mentis and Emovere merged and became one monstrous being. The monster stood in their way and said to Kwaku Ananse, 'I will not allow you to journey with this devil to the god lands. I shall perish when you enter Tumikrom. The vibration of the land shall suck my life from me. When you get to Nyamekrom, you will no longer listen to me before you act. For the god-men listen to the dictates of their hearts and not their lower thoughts and emotions. Don't leave me now, for I have been with you since the very day you fell in love with the animals in Asase. The mountain that you are about to climb shall take you to lands I cannot tread, because of their intense vibrations. Stay with me and enjoy the lower pleasures that I offer you freely.'

Kwaku Ananse said to the monster, 'How ugly you look, Mens Mentis and Emovere. I never knew you were that ugly inside.'

The monster said, 'I am your own creation, Kwaku Ananse. I am ugly because your thoughts and emotions are ugly. The chicken cannot lay the eggs of a dove. I am the accumulation of your lower thoughts and desires. I am already fed up with your insolence. Now turn back before I strike you to the ground.' Kwaku Ananse became terrified by those utterances. When he became terrified, the monster grew in size and in strength. Then Onufu instructed him to be bold.

Kwaku Ananse gained courage and said, 'Get thee behind me, monster, for the hour has come for me to be freed from the prison in which you have enslaved me.' When the monster realized that Kwaku Ananse had gained some courage, it shrunk in size and became weak. Kwaku Ananse broke off a branch from a nearby tree and struck the monster with it. The monster fell to the ground and died.

The three travellers climbed the mountain and mounted the Aerocorn, soaring immediately high into the sky.

The people of Tumikrom waved at them until they disappeared from their sight. The Aerocorn flew higher and higher; eventually, Kwaku Ananse and Aso became unconscious.

Chapter Five

The Green Robe of Odokrom

WHEN KWAKU ANANSE AND Aso regained consciousness, they found themselves in a room of a certain old man who introduced himself as Ziden. Ziden was in his seventies. He wore eyeglasses and a long yellow robe.

Kwaku Ananse and Aso realized they were naked. Ziden gave them each a yellow robe to wear. The robes were silky in texture. Kwaku Ananse and Aso, who were contemplating their new surroundings, remained in silence for a while. They scanned Ziden's room with their eyes. The room contained many books, making it look like a library.

Ziden then spoke. 'Let me get you something to eat.' He left the room and returned with grapes and apples.

Kwaku Ananse and Aso took the fruits, thanked him, and ate them. When they finished eating, Kwaku Ananse asked, 'Who are you, sir?'

Ziden smiled and replied, 'I am your brother in spirit.'

Kwaku Ananse asked, 'What do you mean by "brother in spirit"?

'Being soul siblings means we all evolved out of the same group soul.'

Kwaku Ananse and Aso then said, 'Then we have committed incest!' But Ziden told them not to worry, that incest had no meaning in the language of Odokrom.

'How did you come by all this knowledge?' Aso asked.

Ziden answered, 'You can see I have many books in my room. For a period of over fifty years, I have dedicated my life to seeking the greatest mysteries of all mysteries.'

Kwaku Ananse, remembering their quest, asked, 'Are we in Odokrom?'

'Yes, you are in the first region of the city of Odokrom,' Ziden answered. 'There are seven regions in the city of Odokrom. Let me take you out so that you can witness the majesty of this great city.' Ziden took them out of his room to introduce them to the beautiful city of Odokrom.

The ground of the entire city was covered with chrysanthemum, shamrock, hellebore, green coneflower, and day lily. He told them that in the city of Odokrom, the people didn't pluck fruits from the trees. When you needed fruit, you asked the trees and they gave them to you willingly. Thus, the people only picked fruits from the ground after they had become ripe and fallen naturally.

The animals there were all herbivorous and friendly. Kwaku Ananse and Aso asked Ziden whether he was married, and he told them he had practised celibacy for a period of fifty years. He added that he had also practised vegetarianism during that period of time.

On their way through the city, they met two very short men. Kwaku Ananse asked Ziden, 'Who are these two men?'

'They are the others in the city of Odokrom. They have a different higher self, so they belong to a different nuclear family, although we all belong to the same extended family as human beings. They desire to wear a robe, but they don't know how to sew their own robes; that is why they wear a cloth.'

Continuing their journey, they met another member of the short family wearing a yellow robe. Aso asked Ziden, 'How come this one is wearing a robe?'

He answered, 'His robe was given to him by a member of our nuclear family. Those members of our nuclear family who give robes to the short people do so out of ignorance of the family tree I educated you about.'

Kwaku Ananse asked, 'But why do they carry bowls in their hands?'

'Because they are beggars,' Ziden answered. 'They don't have enough precious fruits like what we have here in our town. I refuse to give them any kind of charity because I don't want to lessen their karmic burden. I want them to learn the harder lessons in life.'

They walked further and soon met two other members of the short family, these wearing green robes. Aso asked Ziden, 'We thought all the robes in this city were yellow in colour; how come these two people wear a green robe?'

Ziden answered, 'You have just witnessed the most unfair thing in the city of Odokrom. The green colour of the robe signifies a transition from Odokrom to the next beautiful city, called Nokorekrom.

'The city of Nokorekrom is the city I desire to transit through in order to get to the great city of Nyamekrom. It is for this reason that I have led a very spiritual life here in Odokrom. Before you can behold the face of our father, you first have to get to the city of Nyamekrom. It is my greatest desire to meet my father. He possesses all the accumulated knowledge gained by his children. He is the wise one who sends his children drops of wisdom and guidance in the form of intuition from time to time.

'I believe I have contributed the greater portion of the accumulated knowledge, yet I have become stuck here in Odokrom. Do you think that is fair? See how these inferior stocks, who cannot even sew their own clothes, are gaining the opportunity to transit through Nokorekrom?'

Kwaku Ananse and Aso then asked Ziden the direction those men were heading towards. He answered, 'They are heading towards the northern side of Odokrom, where a very thick wall separates the city of Odokrom from the city of Nokorekrom. There are sixteen guardians who stand at the sixteen entrances to the city of Nokorekrom. They will only permit those who wear the green robe to pass through their gates into the city of Nokorekrom.'

'But how does one get one of the green robes?' Kwaku Ananse asked.

Ziden answered, 'They claim the yellow robe we wear changes automatically to a green robe the moment one masters the art of unconditional love.'

They asked Ziden whether he knew how to sew the yellow robes and whether he had ever sewn one for the shorter people. He answered that he was perfect in the sewing of the robes but that he would never sew a robe for someone belonging to a different nuclear family.

They got to a point in the city where they saw a very thin wall. Ziden alerted them, saying, 'This is as far as we can get. The entrance in this thin wall leads to the land of the short people.'

Suddenly, they heard a very loud sound like the sound of a bell. Kwaku Ananse and Aso asked, 'What is this loud sound that we hear?'

'The sound you just heard is from the Odokrom Hall of the New Arrivals. It is sounded any time new people arrive from Tumikrom. Let's go and see if they are one of our kind,' Ziden said. They headed towards Odokrom's Hall of Arrival.

When they got to the Hall of Arrival, they saw many people belonging to the two nuclear families of Odokrom gathered at the entrance. They joined them to behold the new arrivals in the hall. There were two Aerocorns there. On top of each of the Aerocorns were two people. Two of them belonged to the Sunsum family, and the other two belonged to the family of the short people. The two Sunsums were Kofi and Ama. They all arrived unconscious. The Sunsums took charge of Kofi and Ama, while the short family took their brother and sister to their land.

Kofi and Ama stayed in the home of Ziden, who gave them yellow robes to wear. When they awoke from their sleep, Ziden took them on a tour through the city of Odokrom. During their tour, they met some members of the short family wearing cloths, and Ziden explained to them that this was because they could not sew their own robes. Kofi and Ama were touched emotionally by the plight of the short family.

As soon as they returned from their tour, Kofi and Ama asked Ziden to teach them how to sew the robes. But they never divulge their secret intention to Ziden, which was to help the short family. When they became perfect in the art, they sewed many of the robes and delivered them as gifts to the short people. They also entered the suburb of Odokrom, where the short people lived, and trained some of them to sew the robes. They occasionally visited them to monitor their progress with the sewing. On the seventh occasion when Kofi and Ama visited the land of the short family to give them further training, their robes turned green the moment they were about to exit through the thin wall that divided the two lands.

They went to their home to say goodbye to Ziden. Ziden was amazed at their robes, and they explained to him what they had done.

Kofi and Ama then headed towards the entrance to the city of Nokorekrom. They were admitted into the city of Nokorekrom after having stayed but one month in the city of Odokrom. Kwaku Ananse and Aso noted their absence, but Ziden chose not to relate what they had told him.

One day, Kwaku Ananse and Aso met two members of the short family wearing green robes and heading towards the city of Nokorekrom. They asked them, 'How did your yellow robes turn green?'

They responded that they didn't know. Kwaku Ananse then asked them to tell them the kind of activities they involved themselves in from day to day in Odokrom. The short people answered, 'Every morning when we wake up, we water the flowers in our family land and those in your family land.

'When we water the flowers belonging to your family land, some of your people try to reward as with expensive gifts like diamonds, but we always reject their presents. We reject the presents because we don't want to be rewarded for doing something we consider to be our duty as human beings. We love the work that we do.

'Despite the fact that Ziden dislikes us, we also water the flowers in his land. We do that when he is asleep, because he shoos us away anytime he sees us around his home.'

Aso asked them, 'Did you do that routinely because you wanted to gain access to the city of Nokorekrom?'

'No!' they answered. 'We did that because we just liked to do that. We don't know so much about God, but the limited knowledge we have about him teaches us that all things are from him. The flowers and the skies are all from him. We consider the invisible things to be his face, and the visible things to be his body or his back. So when we make nature beautiful, we make the body of God beautiful. Out of the love that we have for God, we do what we do.'

Kwaku Ananse and Aso then asked the two short people whether they knew Kofi and Ama. They said they did know them. They also related that Kofi and Ama had taught their people how to sew robes.

Kwaku Ananse and Aso, desiring to enter the city of Nokorekrom, decided to learn how to sew the robes. Ziden trained them in the art. They sewed many robes and delivered them to the members of the short family. They also visited the land of the short family occasionally to train them in the sewing of the robes. They carried out these activities for a period of two years, but their own robes remained yellow.

One day as they walked in a garden in Odokrom, Onufu appeared before Ananse and Asor. Onufu said to Ananse: 'Master, I feel the hour has come for you to kill me. We have been in this city for too long. I don't see any promising sign we might be able to make it to the next city. Maybe this is the end of the journey for you and your partner. I have been blamed for all the evil in your land. Please cut my head and let my body and name be forever buried.'

Ananse and Asor became silent for a very long time. Asor started to cry. Ananse tried to console her. They became so worried about the fact that Odokrom might be the end of their journey and therefore wouldn't have the opportunity to behold the face of their father. Ananse then said to Onufu: 'How can I be better than the devil when I repay his past evil deeds with evil? I have been with you for some time now and I find no fault with you. You haven't done anything evil on our way from the evil forest to this city. Even if you were evil in the past, you have become a better person. I find no reason to use your past to judge your present. You are forgiven Onufu. I shall no longer cut your head as I once told you. The good service you've rendered is enough to compensate for your sins.'

Onufu said to Ananse and Asor: 'in your wisdom, you have tempered justice with mercy; I therefore grant you access to the city of Nokorekrom'. Immediately, the robes of Ananse and Asor turned green.

Ananse and Asor cried out loud: 'Oh, Onufu! So you are the power that carried us from city to city in our quest to become ubiquitous sapiens?' Onufu replied: 'It was the forgiveness in your heart that granted you the robes not I Onufu.'they went home to say good bye to Ziden and headed to the entrance to the city of Nokorekrom which was a green wall without gates. Upon reaching the entrance, one of the guardians asked them: 'for what reason do you approach Nokorekrom, twins? 'To visit the home of our father', they answered.

The guardian spoke again. 'The abode of your father is the abode of perfection. The violet flame is the opportunity that awaits you to transmute your imperfection into perfection. Before you behold the face of your father, you would have to merge to become one in consciousness, like you were before.Are you ready for this great sacrifice?'

They answered in unison. 'We already speak together with one voice, guardian. Ready are we to become whole again'. The guardian asked again: 'tell me how far you have travelled to this very place that you stand?' 'The distance between the stone and the heart', they answered.

'Then you deserve the green robe that you wear, I therefore grant you entry into the city of Nokorekrom. Make sure you articulate your experiences on your way perfectly when you come face to face with the great king and people of Nokorekrom. Else you shall return to this very place with your tails in between your legs', the guardian said.

The guardian then asked them to pass through the thick wall that surrounds the city. Asor then asked the guardian, 'how can we pass through this thick wall'?

The guardian answered: 'you can pass through this thick wall because of the green robe you are wearing'.

Asor asked again, 'why do we need this green robe in order to pass through this thick wall?'

You need this green robe to pass through this wall because the entire region from Asase to Odokrom is under quarantine. We refer to this entire region as the prison world. You cannot leave this region unless you have this green robe. What we refer to as robe you call it body in Asase. 'You didn't attain the new higher bodies by luck if I may use your language. It was through unconditional love, humility, selfless service and forgiveness that you were able to build the higher bodies you now wear. Waste no more time my beloved friends, your father will answer any more questions you may have. Please enter the wall now.'

Ananse and Asor with Onufu passed through the green thick wall of Odokrom.

Chapter Six

The Flaming Sword of Nokorekrom

KWAKU ANANSE AND ASO, with Onufu, entered the beautiful city of Nokorekrom in the afternoon. The city floor was covered with beautiful flowers, including anemone, skyflower, blue flag iris, pitcher sage, autumn sage, germander sage, blue lithospermum, and annual lobelia.

When the people of Nokorekrom saw the party entering their city, they ran to their king's palace to await the speech that the party would deliver before their king so that they would be granted access to awaken in the next city of Nyamekrom.

Ananse and Asor appeared before the great king of Nokorekrom who was sitting on a white elephant. The majesty of his palace could not be described in words. They were offered water to drink, and then the king said to them, 'You are welcome in the city of Nokorekrom. May we know the reason that brings you to our city?'

Kwaku Ananse replied thus: 'We are pilgrims returning to the home of our father. We have come to your city not to seek residence but to transit to the next city of Nyamekrom.'

The great king laughed and said, 'Your accent betrays you as the extensions of Nyamekitua. How long it has taken you to dream in the Hall of Knowledge. Well, the fact that you stand here indicates that your period of dreaming is coming to an end. You are no longer called dreamers. For he who dreams and knows not that he dreams is the dreamer. The quest that you seek before me is to be given the opportunity to awaken in the Great Hall of Resurrection.

'Neither sound nor touch can awaken he who is in a coma in the Great Hall of Knowledge. It is only the agony of the violet flame that awakens a man in the Great Hall of Resurrection. However, the violet flame is guarded by the flaming sword. And he who is not judged worthy

by the flaming sword shall not be permitted by the sword, which wields
its own power, to meet the terror in the violet flame.

'How far have you travelled, grandchildren of Nyamekitua?'

'From the stone to Nokorekrom, my lord,' Aso answered.

Suddenly, a voice echoed among the crowd: 'Great king, let them
articulate their observations in their way, that we may know that what
they speak before our king is the truth.'

The king then said, 'Kwaku Ananse! The people of Nokorekrom
desire to know what you saw on your way from the stone to our land.
For no one who speaks untruth shall be allowed to approach the flaming
sword. Such a person shall be struck like thunder to return to the stone,
by the power that the sword wields. From the smoke of burning wood,
we shall determine its name.'

With a loud voice, Kwaku Ananse started speaking.

'A turkey vulture that dislikes a foul smell shall be disowned by its
family.

'A lion that fears a multitude of prey shall die of hunger.

'A pilgrim who fears evil knows not his destination.

'The quality of the human voice should not be measured by the
quantity of the vocal cords that produce it.

'He who fears reproach cannot speak against the vox populi.

'That which causes our fear is not outside us but is within us.

'I saw a man who was chased by a dog in the morning, but he chased
that same dog in the afternoon under the influence of wine.

'I also saw a big dog that chased a small fowl every morning but was
chased in turn the very day the fowl hatched its chicks.

'A young hawk that fears to fly from its nest cannot testify to the
sweetness of the chick.

'He who fears to endure pain should be served uncooked rice soaked
in cold water, and not cooked rice.

'When an aphid advises you not to spray your plant with garlic spray, demand a reason. When it answers that it's because garlic spray is not good for plants, demand a further reason.

'A hawk that falls in love with an owl chooses between his life and his heart.

'That which you call disaster is the signpost that directs you to your destination.

'The events that shake the foundation of your life are the steps of the ladder you climb to the top of your mountain.

'Never determine the gender of an experience till it is nine months old.

'He who blesses comfort and curses suffering should also curse the night that gave him a place to dream about the comfort that he blesses.

'Those who have eyes learn through the eyes. And those who have ears learn through their ears. But those who are blind and dumb learn through bitter experience.

'God created man and woman. Man and woman created comfort and suffering, then comfort and suffering begat progress and knowledge.

'Eating the fruit of bitterness is not punishment, but a lesson to teach how to sow a good seed today and tomorrow.

'He who hates his wife but loves his children is a man who hates fire but drinks porridge.

'Comfort is the sugar we put in our tea in the morning, and suffering is the salt we put in our soup in the evening. Together, they help us to function as humans.

'Light would have to give way to darkness before the sky could impregnate Asase, supplying enough semen to give birth to fertility.

'The very thing that the cow considers waste is considered to be fresh and nutritious by the plant.

'The plant that ate the waste of the cow was in turn eaten by the same cow, who later produced milk for man and his children.

'Suffering is the bitter seed we sowed yesterday, and comfort is the charity we gave yesterday.

'He who causes tears to flow from his brother's eyes should be prepared to clean those tears from his own face tomorrow. For what you do unto others is what you ask the powers of the universe to do unto you tomorrow.

'The carnivorous exist not to bring the existence of the herbivorous to an end but rather to preserve their existence.

'Balance is the name of the guardian who preserves the life of creation.

'I was asked to count the number of barren women in the world, so I counted the number of orphans in the world. Ignorance is the veil that separates the orphan and the barren woman. In their prayers, the orphan desires the return of his own mother, and the barren woman desires the fruit of her own womb.

'Balance is the soil in which the seed of evolution thrives.

'In all things, give thanks unto the Lord, for the negative and positive polarities are the parent of evolution.

'Learn to walk the middle path and you shall become immortal like the stone, which is neither dead nor alive.

'Many are those who preach about love and unity but find it difficult to practise that which they preach.

'And many are those who give charity to a God they do not see but refuse to give a crumb of bread to the needy they always see.

'He who walks the path of Ziden shall be blind to the face of his Father.

'Selfishness is the veil that blocks the sight from beholding the face of God.

'When all plants decide to be selfish, what shall become the fate of men?

'Out of ignorance the fool constantly sings in his heart that the universe was created for his sustenance. He sings the same song as the germ in his body, which thinks the body of the fool was created for its sustenance. Together they dance the dance of selfishness and sing the chorus of ignorance. And out of their dance and chorus, disease is born.

'Let the oil palm tree be your greatest teacher in giving and in being humble. She gave her branches for shelter, her fruit for food, and her leaves for a broom, without expecting a reward. Despite her generosity, she was insulted and felled to the ground. Even in death, she didn't stop giving. She continued to give to the wise man who knew how to prepare palm wine from her sap. Learn to be humble like her, and the wise shall think you foolish. In their wisdom, they shall become overjoyed. And in their over-enjoyment, they shall dance the dance of a fool. And through that, they shall display their folly to the world.

'Diversity is the dress that God wears to cover his nakedness, which is oneness.

'It takes unconditional love, through divine wisdom, to uncover the nakedness of God if one desires to realize his true reality.

'He who has knowledge but lacks love is like the atheist who dreams but does not believe in the supernatural.

'In the eyes of men you may be called wise. But in the eyes of God you are a fool, because true wisdom enables you to realize the oneness of all things.

'And the knowledge of unity in diversity should lead one to love unconditionally. For a God-realized soul is one who loves unconditionally and not one who gains all the knowledge in the world but fails to see through the thin veil of illusion with his heart.

'He who needs love should seek the needy, and he shall find love. For in giving you shall receive.

'Behind every thin veil lives the greatest desire of your heart. He who can see through the veil of thinness shall receive the greatest treasure from love. Seeing through the thin veil with the eyes of love gives us the strength to break down the thick wall that separates us from our greatest heart's desire.

'It is the smallest deeds we dispense with love that give us the strength to accomplish the greater things our strength alone cannot overcome.

'When we water the little seed with the water of love, we shall surely see a big tree in its place in the future.

'Charity is the scale used by the Almighty to measure the weight of every heart.

'As unique as we are, so is the uniqueness of the scale used to measure every heart.

'The living things around us are mirrors in which we see the beauty of our hearts. When we see God in the mirror, we see God in our hearts. When we see God in our hearts, we feel God in our hearts. And when we feel God in our heart, we give abundantly without receiving or expecting a reward.

'Never discriminate against a person by the amount of melanin their melanocytes produces. For the root of hate is ignorance.

'Measure not my wealth by what I have but by what I have invested in the hearts of the underprivileged.

'Let the ant be your greatest teacher of intuition. Out of envy and ignorance, the fool takes a stick and breaks down the anthill. He cries in his heart, how can small ants be that intelligent? They will recognize me as their master because I have given them an assignment to accomplish. What assignment do they have to accomplish when the magnificence of their accomplishment lies hidden beneath the surface of Asase and when that which the fool destroyed is the mere shadow of their intelligence? The ant travels a long distance to take a grain of sugar from the fool's table. The fool, instead of honouring the intelligence of the ant and being kind to it by giving it additional sugar, crushes it with his finger and cries in his heart, asking, "How come a small creature like you is that devilish? How did you know there was an unwanted grain of sugar on my table? You steal food to save your family, yet you cannot save your own self." He is the very person who would die in the desert because he would fail to find an oasis a few metres away from where his now dead body lies.

'I overheard a conversation between the sun and a beautiful tree one afternoon. The tree asked the sun, "Why do you keep giving me energy without receiving anything in return?" The sun answered, "It's because I'm in love with you." The tree asked, "If you love me, why don't you feel jealous when men pluck my fruits?" The sun answered, "It's because I don't feel I own you." The tree asked, "If you love me, why don't you feel pain when they take my fruits to their homes?" The sun answered, "It's because I don't feel attached to you." The tree asked, "If you love me, why don't you get angry and strike them? Instead you smile when you see them eating my fruit in their homes." The sun answered with a question: "How can I get angry when I don't feel pain?" The tree concluded, "Your love is pure, selfless, and beneficial. Divine is your love, O sun!"

'Detachment should become an emotional exercise and not a physical exercise.

'Power is like the salt that you put into your food to give it a good taste. When you apply too little or too much, inefficiency is born. For neither dry land nor excessive water is appropriate for the cultivation of rice.

'Asase is a good mother and shall provide for all the needs of her children. She is the soil in which you, the seed, are sown to mature before you are cultivated by the hands of the Almighty. Learn to see her beautiful face and love her like you love your human mother, and then she will speak to you through all living things. She has blessed the animals with good health because they have taken the place of men as her faithful children. Man, who claims to be the most intelligent among her children, uses his sweat and toil to produce weapons to destroy his fellow men and their Mother Nature.

'You have elected blind people as your leaders. They waste your efforts in vanities and steal from your coffers.

'You have elected the blind to drive you to your destination. May you have a safe journey!

'You have created artificial boundaries to satisfy your selfishness.

'You kill and destroy in the name of God. When did God appoint you as judges to occupy his throne?

'Out of ignorance, you have created chaos in the world. When did God grant you authority to kill on his behalf?

'You sinners who sin a hundred times a day and seek forgiveness a hundred times a day destroy your fellows to deny them repentance.

'The fool wastes his lifetime in evil practices and foolishly thinks himself the soldier of Almighty God.

'You have divided the resources of the world among yourself and have allowed your impoverished siblings to suffer.

'You have created systems to protect your selfishness, and you have become slaves to your own creations.

'Remove your dark eyeglasses and you shall see the world clearly.'

Once Kwaku Ananse had drawn his speech to a close, the king spoke: 'You have indeed journeyed from silence to our land. You have passed the test of truth-speaking, and as a result you have proven yourself worthy of wearing the blue robe of Nokorekrom.'

Two blue robes were given to Kwaku Ananse and Aso to replace the green robes they had worn from Odokrom. After they put on their new attire, the king spoke again. 'The flaming sword awaits you at the great entrance that leads to the Hall of Resurrection in the city of Nyamekrom.'

The high priest of Nokorekrom escorted Kwaku Ananse and Aso, together with Onufu, to the entrance that led to the city of Nyamekrom. At the border that divided the cities of Nyamekrom and Nokorekrom, they saw two gates leading to the city of Nyamekrom, one on the left and the other on the right. The one on the left was known as the Gate of Return. Beyond this gate was the violet flame. And in front of the gate was a flaming sword that hung in the air, guarding the entrance.

The gate on the right was the Gate of Service. This was the gate for the servicemen who moved into and out of Nyamekrom.

When they came close to the flaming sword, the high priest stood back and said, 'I believe you have already started feeling the power that the flaming sword wields now that you are merging with its aura.'

Kwaku Ananse and Aso began to tremble on their feet. The high priest shouted with great power in his voice: 'Carefully hold the handle. Kwaku Ananse, hold with your right palm, and you, Aso, do so with your left palm.' They did as instructed. Their bodies began to shake with the intense vibration. Onufu then moved to join them, and with his help they regained some strength in their legs. Immediately, the Gate of Return opened. They saw the violet flame glowing inside it. The high priest continued his instruction. 'Now point the edge towards the sky and confidently walk into the violet flame.

'Make sure you don't look back, for you have already taken the first step. And I believe you know the consequences of such a cowardly action. Move now, Kwaku Ananse and Aso, for the time has come for you to awaken from your slumber!'

Kwaku Ananse and Aso entered the flame with Onufu. Once they had entered, the Gate of Return closed. That was the end of their individuality as Kwaku Ananse and Aso, and that was also the end of Onufu, the Evil One, who sacrificed his life to give power to Kwaku Ananse and Aso so that they could pass through the violet flame of Nyamekrom.

Chapter Seven

Akwaaba to Nyamekrom

THE BEAUTIFUL LAND of Nyamekrom was covered with the flowers Baptisia australis, brantwood, and bellflower dalmatian. There were two great halls in the city. One was the Hall of Knowledge, at the eastern side of Nyamekrom, and the other was the Hall of Resurrection, at the western side.

The Great Hall of Knowledge had an entrance but no exit of its own. However, the Great Hall of Resurrection was mysteriously linked to the Great Hall of Knowledge as the latter's exit point. This was a great mystery that the inhabitants of Nyamekrom found difficult to understand.

The Great Hall of Knowledge had two chambers within it. These chambers were known as the Chamber of Knowledge and the Chamber of Service. Inside the Chamber of Knowledge lay the bodies of multitudes of people who were in a deep coma-like sleep. This was why some residents of Nyamekrom referred to the Chamber of Knowledge as the Chamber of Coma. And the Chamber of Service was also known as the Chamber of Rest because it contained the perfected ones who rested their bodies inside so that they could serve in the lower cities, such as Asase and Ewiase.

Kwaku Ananse came face to face with his father called Nyamekitua. He informed Nyamekitua about his desire to find the Devil.

Nyamekitua laughed out loud and said, 'Look inside the crystal ball. I will reveal to you the true devil causing your problems.' A series of scenes from Asase appeared in the crystal ball, revealing the true identity of the devil causing the problems in Asase.

Kwaku Ananse bowed his head and wept. He remained silent for a long time, later saying, 'I have found who this mysterious devil is. I am going back to my people to reveal to them who this devil is.'

Chapter Eight

The Return of Kwaku Ananse

ON A BRIGHT DAY IN the afternoon, seven women were carrying water jugs containing water they had fetched from river Asase. Suddenly two dogs accompanying the women started backing. Some nearby roosters also started crowing. 'Have they seen a snake'? One of the women asked. One of the women immediately turned her gaze towards the direction to which the dogs were barking. To her amazement she spotted Ananse appearing from the Evil forest.

The woman dropped her water jug, which fell from her head to the ground, and shouted very loud, 'Eeei, Kwaku Ananse.' The remaining six women also shouted the name of Kwaku Ananse and dropped their water jugs to the ground. The women then ran into their main village shouting the name of Kwaku Ananse.

Within a period of one hour, every one of the villagers of Asase had assembled at the meeting grounds in front of the chief's palace. Kwaku Ananse headed to the palace and was hugged by the chief and the elders. He was given water in a calabash by the Queen Mother herself and then was given a stool to sit on.

The chief without delay asked Kwaku Ananse, 'How are you able to return so soon? It was some days ago that you left us to pursue the Devil. Was it fear that drove you back, or was hope and good news the legs that returned you sooner?'

Kwaku Ananse narrated his experiences from Asase to the garden in the evil forest.

The chief inquired of Kwaku Ananse, "Share with us the revelation about this devil in the land of the gods."

Kwaku Ananse addressed his people, recounting a tale: "A leader seeks a loan abroad, ostensibly to aid his people in times of hardship. Yet, upon receiving the funds, he and his officials conspire, dividing the money for personal gain and election campaigns, neglecting crucial development projects. The blame is shifted to the Devil as the impoverished citizens suffer. Who, then, is the devil?

As elections approach, leaders drain national coffers for campaigns, leaving the country impoverished afterward. The blame is placed on the Devil once more. Incompetent party donors gain positions, hindering progress. Blame again falls on the Devil.

Foreign nations exploit the resources of poorer nations, causing continued poverty. Corrupt leaders profit from unfavorable deals, with the Devil shouldering the blame. Institutions favor family over competence, leading to unemployment, blamed on the Devil.

A focus on education results in a surplus of graduates, but limited job opportunities, prompting blame on the Devil. Poor nations rely on imports, overlooking the potential of local production, and poverty persists. The Devil is blamed.

Overpopulation in poor families leads to struggles, with the Devil as the scapegoat. Free energy on Asase is suppressed, perpetuating economic enslavement. Gaia's abundant land is sold at a high price, blaming the Devil for costly living.

A poor family loses their land, leading to a life of poverty, blamed on the Devil. Elephants are slaughtered for their ivory, and humanity values money over life. Who, then, is the Devil?

A priest exploits a woman, and poor girls working overseas suffer abuse, with blame placed on the Devil. Nations compete in nuclear weapons, raising questions about wisdom. An innocent child is molested by a priest, who faces no consequences, leading to psychological trauma.

In the midst of such realities, Kwaku Ananse raised challenging questions about who truly bears the blame. The priest, angered, attempted to silence him, invoking blasphemy. However, Ananse urged his people to awaken from ignorance, revealing the Mesopotamian Civilization as the first, dispelling myths about angels and gods, and unveiling the truth about ancient knowledge suppressed by the dark cabal.

As Ananse attempted to enlighten his people, the King intervened, banishing him to the Evil Forest. Ananse left with a final message about the Magisterial Mission.Space ships appeared in the skies and a flying saucer descended and picked Ananse."

Chapter Nine

The New Age

IN AN UNFAMILIAR ENVIRONMENT beneath Asase's surface, Kwaku Ananse discovered himself in the company of various beings. Taken to a meticulously prepared office, he learned for the first time that he was destined to be the new leader of the planet Asase. A tour of his unique surroundings revealed a bustling community of humans and beings from other universes, including the industrious Greyman Beings.

Ushered onto his throne, Kwaku Ananse assumed the role of Asase's Messiah. A televised broadcast reached every corner of the globe, causing widespread confusion. Some hailed him as a savior, while others labeled him the Antichrist.

Amidst the global uncertainty, nations were called to unite under a single government led by Kwaku Ananse. Remarkable individuals were recruited, and those opposing the new order faced intervention from the Grey aliens, now the enforcers of the New Age.

Initially, chaos ensued, but over time, a profound transformation occurred. Lasting peace and happiness prevailed as weapons of mass destruction and their manufacturing facilities were obliterated. A new map replaced the old, talents were embraced, and humans coexisted harmoniously with the Greyman Beings.

The fusion of nations brought about a unified currency, eradicating religions in favor of a new spiritual science focused on the connection between humanity and the inner spirit. Asase joined a confederation of planets, welcoming beings from distant worlds.

The era of wars and conflicts between nations and tribes vanished, enabling unrestricted movement across Asase without visas. Thus, the New Age dawned, extinguishing the old world of greed, domination, environmental destruction, and war, ushering in an era of unity and peace.

.

Don't miss out!

Visit the website below and you can sign up to receive emails whenever Richard Kofi Armah publishes a new book. There's no charge and no obligation.

https://books2read.com/r/B-A-DDHDB-TDRVC

Connecting independent readers to independent writers.